Everybody makes mistakes

Table of Content

Introduction

Whether you're reading aloud or your kids read for themselves, these fun, creative stories teach something important: that it's okay to make mistakes. The tales include mistakes involving a mermaid's fashion, a superhero who saves animals, an older brother's art and a singing princess. Each story shows that it's okay to not be perfect; that you can always learn from mistakes. And, in some cases, a mistake might even make something better. To add to the fun, each story has pictures for your child to color in, making it a more interactive experience!

Even Moms and Dads Make Mistakes

Pete sniffed the delicious smells coming from the kitchen. He walked in to see his dad, as usual, cooking at the stove. "Mmm, what's for dinner?" Pete asked as he eyed the steaming pots and pans.

His dad pointed a spoon to the bigger pot. "Freshly made pasta and my super-duper, world-famous spicy meatballs," he said, trying to sound like a TV show announcer.

This made Pete smile broadly, both at his dad's silly voice and the fact that he really was going to eat the best pasta with spicy meatballs in the world. His dad hadn't been joking about that part! Pete's dad wasn't just great at cooking, but at baking treats too. Just then, Pete's younger sister, Dee, twirled in like a ballerina, wearing her pink tutu over pants. His mom came in too.

"Guess what?" Dee clasped her hands together, "Mom's taking me and my friend to a real ballet this week! And she's going to buy me a special sparkly purple dress to wear!"

Their dad turned from where he stirred the meatballs. "That's great Dee. It's an exciting week because Grandma's big birthday party is this Friday. And I'm making my super special, triple-layer chocolate cake!"

Dee giggled. "Goody, I love cake!"

Pete smiled as he set the table. "Me too, and the chocolate triple layer is your best one yet, dad."

As his dad sprinkled oregano into the sauce he nodded. "Why thank you, I agree, it is my best!" Moments later, the four of them sat down and had the amazing meal, ending with his dad's mouth-watering blueberry pie.

***

Pete ran as fast as his legs would take him and… kick… whoosh! The soccer ball sailed through the air right to his teammate, Juan. And then Juan, who was lined up before the goal, kicked it straight into the net! "Goooaal!" Juan and Pete cried together, giving each other a high-five. His other teammates came over too, cheering.

Pete saw his mom jumping up and down on the sidelines calling out, "Nice pass Pete, and good shot Juan!" Pete grinned over at his mom. She always came to his games, and went to Dee's ballet recitals. His mom also worked from home, did bake sales for school and many other things. She was super organized, keeping track of the whole family's schedule every week.

It was Thursday evening before dinner, and the day before grandma's party. Pete's dad chopped veggies for a stew while his mom sat at the counter with her daily planner and pen. "So, Dee has a recital this Saturday at 2pm, and Pete, you have a game on Sunday, right?"

Pete nodded. "Yup, at 4pm coach said." His mom scribbled this down into the planner.

"And the bake sale is tomorrow right after school," his mom continued, talking half to herself. "So, I'll have to hurry to get the balloons and decorations for grandma's party after the sale."

His dad pushed all the chopped veggies into a pot and said, "Okay, and I've got all the food covered. Grandma's favorite lasagna and, of course, the triple layer chocolate cake."

Mom smiled. "Perfect!" Then she tapped her pen on her chin. "Oh, and I'm going to get Dee's purple dress to wear to both the birthday party and the ballet. Is there anything else to add to the planner?"

Pete and his dad looked at each other, then at her and shrugged. "I don't think so," Dad said.

"Yeah, I think you got it all Mom," Pete said.

"In that case, good," his mom said. "I can relax and get ready to eat this amazing stew soon!" She closed the planner firmly.

It was late afternoon the next day, Friday. And Pete was helping his dad prepare for Grandma's birthday. "She's coming in about an hour," Dad said, "and your mom's coming with decorations in about twenty minutes. Can you take a look at the lasagna to see if it's ready?"

Pete walked by his dad who was cracking eggs into the cake batter. Carefully pulling the oven open, he peeked inside. "I think it's ready," Pete told his dad. "The cheese on top is golden brown."

Dad let out a breath. "Whew, good, and that's right, it's ready." Dad came over with oven mitts to take the lasagna out, "I've taught you well son!" Pete beamed.

"Now, I have just enough time to bake the cake before grandma comes. We'll have to keep her out of the kitchen so it's a surprise."

As Pete passed by his dad again, he looked into the cake batter bowl while his dad added sugar. "Can I have a taste?" Pete's finger reached out, but his dad lightly swatted it away with a smile.

"Absolutely not. Grandma gets first taste, so no batter tasting!"

Pete laughed. "Okay, okay, I'll just wait."

Over the next hour, Pete and his parents decorated the place and the cake came out of the oven to cool and frost. Dee came down wearing her light purple sparkly dress Mom had bought. As Dee swirled in her dress into the living room, their mom came out at the exact same time with a huge bowl of red fruit punch. Neither one saw the other until it was too late.

CRASH!!

"Ooo, that's cold!" Dee cried as the punch spilled over her and her dress.

"Oh Dee, sorry!" their mom exclaimed as she managed to hold onto the glass bowl and stop the punch from spilling over. She put the punch on the table where other food stood as Dee looked down at her dress. Her bottom lip began to quiver right as a ding-dong sounded from the front door. Dad went to answer it and greet Grandma and Pete's aunt and uncle, while Mom went to kneel in front of Dee with bunches of napkins.

"Oh sweetie, your dress," Mom said as she patted at the red stains. "I don't think this is going to come out. You'll have to change for the party."

Tears began to spill down Dee's round cheeks. "Y... you can't get the stain out?" Dee's voice squeaked. "B... but I was going to wear it to the ballet show tomorrow! I even have the hair bow to match the dress and everything was going to be perfect!" Pete watched with wide eyes as his little sister ran off to the downstairs bathroom, crying.

Pete's mom gave him a pleading look. "Pete, could you go talk to Dee? Tell her I'll make it up to her and buy her a new dress. I have to greet Grandma and the others and finish getting everything ready." Pete nodded and hurried to talk to Dee.

"Dee, can I come in?" Pete asked, pushing at the partly opened bathroom door. She was at the sink wiping at tears. She just shrugged, not looking at him. "Mom says she's going to get you a new dress tomorrow," Pete told her gently. "It was all an accident – a mistake. She didn't mean to spill punch on your dress."

Dee looked up at Pete. "But she never spills things or makes mistakes," Dee sniffled. "And now my favorite dress in the whole world is wrecked!"

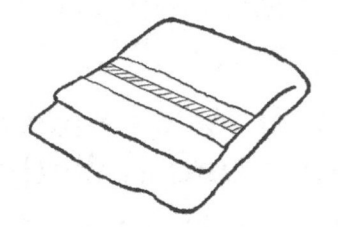

Pete took a washcloth, got it wet with cold water and dabbed at his little sister's face. "I know, I'm sorry sis. But it's okay. I guess even moms make mistakes sometimes. And you can go change into another pretty dress for now." A moment later, Dee looked a little less sad, went to change into a deep green dress and came to sit with Pete at the dinner table. They had a great lasagna dinner and their mom came back saying sorry to everyone, including Dee, again.

Dee still looked a little grumpy but managed to give Grandma a big birthday hug and smile.

"And now, time for cake!" Pete's dad clapped his hands together as his mom lowered the lights.

"Oh wonderful!" Grandma exclaimed. "I love your triple-layer chocolate cake!"

They all sang, "Happy birthday to you… happy birthday to you…" Then Grandma blew out the candles and Dad cut a hug piece of cake for her. He also got everyone else a piece. Pete sat down in front of his cake as Grandma picked up her fork.

"I wish I could just eat the whole piece right now with my hands!" he thought. It smelled sooo good.

"Wait for Grandma to take the first bite, remember kids!" Their dad smiled and wagged a finger at Pete and Dee.

They waited patiently as Grandma got a big bite on her

fork and raised it to her mouth. She ate the bite and chewed. Pete was about to eat his first bite too when he noticed Grandma stopped chewing as her gray eyebrows furrowed. "Um..." grandma said frowning down at the cake.

Then Dee piped up, her mouth full of a bite now too. "Why does it taste so funny?" Dad's eyebrows went up and he took a bite just as Pete decided to try it as well.

He chewed and then stopped right away. It wasn't very sweet - more salty and bitter. "Oh no," his dad said, "I must've put salt instead of sugar in the batter and even the frosting!" His dad looked from Pete to his mom and then Grandma. "Sorry Mom," he told Pete's grandma. "Our new salt and sugar containers look almost the same. I ruined your cake." His grandma looked from his dad down to the cake, mouth in a straight line.

"Oh no, is grandma mad about this?" Pete wondered worriedly. But then Grandma's mouth turned up and she burst out laughing. She laughed so hard tears streamed from her eyes. This got his dad and mom to start laughing too. And then Pete's aunt and uncle... and finally, Pete, and even Dee, began to giggle too.

When the laughter died down, Grandma smiled at Pete's dad, "Honey, thank you."

His dad tilted his head. "For what? I ruined your birthday cake."

She beamed at him. "True, but I don't care about that. And it's the thought that counts. Besides, I haven't laughed that hard in a good while!" That caused another round of laughter. And Pete's grandma ended up having a wonderful rest of her birthday with brownies instead of cake, then balloons and presents.

Everyone had left and Pete, Dee and their parents started to clean up. Pete stood next to his little sister, drying dishes. Then he looked from their mom to their dad and leaned down to whisper to Dee, "I guess dads make mistakes sometimes too, not just moms." He smiled and Dee giggled as she looked at their dad.

"Yeah, I guess you're right! And maybe I'll love my new dress even more than the purple one." And it was true. The next day, Mom got Dee an even prettier, yellow and white dress with even more sparkles.

But for that Friday evening, Pete continued drying dishes and thought to himself, "I guess it's okay to make mistakes. Mom and Dad both did, and it seemed bad at first. But they both ended up just fine, apologizing and then having fun anyway!"

Even Superheroes Make Mistakes

Leo reached for the next tree branch, trying to climb higher. He was in the town park with his friend, Oliver. He used all his arm and leg muscles to pull himself to the next branch. Then he had to pause to catch his breath. "I wish I could climb as fast as Super Sam," Leo called down to Oliver.

"No one can climb as fast as him," Oliver replied, climbing up next to Leo.

"And no one can hear and understand animals who need rescuing from so far away like Super Sam," Leo added with a glimmer in his eyes. Super Sam was a young man in their town who wore a forest green outfit and a dark green mask just around his eyes. He was always in the news, showing how he'd rescued a cat from a tree or a sea turtle from a net in the lake.

He helped save animals nearly every day. It helped that Super Sam had a super speedy ability to climb trees or lampposts, kind of like a monkey or a squirrel.

Leo looked up in the higher tree branches and spotted a nest. "I'm going to go higher and check out that nest," Leo told Oliver. "Maybe some birds need rescuing!"

"Good idea," Oliver agreed.

Leo climbed up carefully. He wasn't as quick as a monkey. But he made it to the nest and peered inside. There were three little light blue eggs. "Robin's eggs," he called down to his friend. "I guess they don't need rescuing and… Agh!" Just then, the mommy Robin swooped down into the top of the tree, flapping her wings and twittering angrily. "S… Sorry," Leo told the bird, "I'm not trying to hurt your eggs!"

The mommy Robin, of course, didn't understand Leo. She thought he was trying to steal or eat her babies inside the eggs! So, she landed close to Leo's face and twittered even louder and fiercer. Leo got so scared he lost his grip and fell! "Ow, umph!" he screamed out as his arm scraped along a branch and his legs got bumped and bruised.

"Leo!" Oliver called, luckily not in the path of Leo's fall.

Leo reached out and managed to hold onto the lowest branch before hitting the ground. He swung, like a monkey this time, and then eased himself onto the ground. Oliver was next to him in the next moment. "Are you okay?" he asked.

Leo examined his scraped arm and bumped legs. Then he shook it off. "I'm fine," he replied. "You know, maybe Super Sam fell from trees and got bumps when he was first starting too."

Oliver thought about this. "Maybe he did, but maybe he was always really good."

Leo frowned and shoved him playfully. "Hey, you're not helping me feel any better!"

They both laughed a little, then Oliver said, "Let's go get ice cream from the park cart. That will make you feel better."

Leo grinned. "Definitely – race you!" And they were off.

That night, Leo sat watching the evening news with his parents after dinner. "Oh, look Leo," his dad said, "Super Sam is on." Leo leaned forward in his seat as the TV showed a clip of Super Sam. The hero was climbing the side of a two-story house in the town. A fire blazed on the first floor and was going up the house. And a dog was barking out of a second-floor window!

"The poor dog," his mom exclaimed.

"It's okay," Leo said, eyes never leaving the TV screen. "Sam will save it!" And sure enough, with nimble climbing, Sam reached the dog, got it in one arm and climbed down to the ground. The house owners had been away for dinner and didn't know about the fire. And now they went to hug their dog and Sam as well.

"We can't thank you enough for rescuing our Sparky," the woman owner gushed to Sam. "You're amazing!"

The older man owner nodded and asked, "And you could really hear our dog from far away?"

Sam smiled, "I was about ten blocks away and, yes, I could hear Sparky's distressed bark. I could understand that he was calling for help, and I came as quickly as I could."

"Incredible",

the man said.

After more thanks, the news reporter turned to Super Sam. "You've done it again Sam, you're the town's own actual superhero," the woman reporter beamed. "I still don't understand how you can climb so well. When did that start?"

Sam looked a little bashful. "Since I was a boy. But I never knew why." He shrugged.

Leo sighed. "He was a boy when he got the ability. He was probably born with it," he thought. "But I'm still going to try and get better at climbing, and animal rescuing!"

All that week Leo practiced. He practiced listening for animals 'talking': bird calls, mice squeaks, frog chirps and even crickets singing. He couldn't tell if they were in distress, but he was aware of them. And he practiced climbing. He climbed anything, from trees to drainpipes on his house to a rope swing in Oliver's back yard.

"I think I'm getting better," Leo told Oliver as he came down from the top of the rope swing one day.

"Yeah, you really are," his friend agreed. "Now you just need to rescue an animal without messing up." Oliver grinned playfully and Leo frowned.

"Yeah, I need to not mess up like with the dog and mouse."

Leo had tried to rescue a dog from the side of a busy

road. But he ended up scaring it away. And then there was a mouse with its tail in a mouse trap in an alley near the town café. Leo had ended up hurting the mouse's tail more than it already was, by accident. But he was still determined to rescue an animal. Even if it was an ant or a butterfly.

So, the next day, after cooling himself in his backyard pool from the summer heat, Leo went to the town park. He had his eyes and ears on high alert. "I hear birds chirping happily," he said softly to himself. "Kids playing in the playground, dogs barking for fun and…" He paused. There was a "meow-meoooooww," coming from somewhere to the right.

Leo's eyes went big as he followed the sound into a large cluster of trees. "That's definitely a cat in distress!" Leo told himself. He looked up a tree to, indeed, see a white cat on a high branch, stuck there! He moved through a few bushes around the tree where some butterflies flew. Then he started to put his improved climbing skills to use. He wasn't as quick as Super Sam, but he did a good job getting to the cat's branch.

"Hey there," he said in a calm, soft voice. "It's okay, I'll help you get down. Just relax, okay?" Leo reached for the cat but she didn't relax, not at all. In fact, she seemed to get more alarmed as Leo's one arm reached for her.

"Meoooooww – Hisssss!" the cat cried at Leo. But Leo managed to get and arm around the smaller cat and started to climb down.

"It's okay, I'm helping," he said to the cat as he got closer to the ground.

But as he was almost down, the cat let out a great hiii-isss baring her teeth and then dug her claws into Leo's arm! "Oww!" Leo cried as he let the cat go. She landed on the ground, on her feet as cats always do, and ran off. Leo fell backward and landed with his back in the bushes!

"Umph!" he cried. Dizzily, he stood and rubbed his back. It hadn't been that far to the ground, but it had hurt a bit. "Well, at least I rescued the cat, even if I got scratched and bumped," he thought.

But then he saw two butterflies on the ground. Each one had a smashed wing and couldn't seem to fly. Leo's forehead creased. "Oh no, I hurt the butterflies!" Tears pricked behind his eyes as he scooped them up.

"Come on, you can still fly, right guys?" he asked the butterflies. And they both did fly after several minutes, but not very well. Leo felt a lump in his throat as he went home. "I saved the cat, but hurt the butterflies," he mumbled to himself in his room. "I'm just not cut out to be a superhero like Sam. I'm messing up too much."

For days, Leo felt down. He didn't try to listen for animals in distress or practice climbing. He didn't try to save anyone or anything. Then, one late afternoon in the park as he rode his scooter alone, Leo saw Super Sam! Leo could hardly believe his eyes as he saw the green-masked man hurry into a patch of trees. No one else saw Sam, only Leo, who followed him under the tree branches.

"I don't want to get in the way, but I have to see. He's going to rescue an animal, I'm sure!" he thought excitedly. He stood back and watched as Super Sam gently scooped two baby birds who had fallen from their nest. "There, there, I'll get you back home," Sam whispered to the birds. Then, one-handed, Sam climbed the tree. It was just as fast and amazing as it looked on TV. He put the birds in the nest and started to climb back down.

But just then, a loud caw of a crow sounded, and Sam

looked up in surprise. Sam's right foot slipped on a branch and he fell! Leo wouldn't have believed it if he hadn't been there watching with his own two eyes! "Oof!" Sam called out as he landed on a big dirt hill on the ground.

"Are you okay?" Leo asked, rushing forward.

Sam looked at the boy in surprise. "Oh, I didn't see you there," Sam said as he stood up.

Leo's cheeks turned pink as he got close to the young man dressed in green. "I, um, saw you head over here and came to watch. Did you get hurt? What happened to make you fall? I thought you never fell?" Leo couldn't stop the questions from popping out of his mouth. Sam smiled, eyes glittering behind the mask.

"I got a little distracted by the crow cawing," he said. "And I do indeed fall sometimes, I'm not perfect."

He looked down to the hill of dirt he'd smashed on his fall. "Oh no, I even smashed this ant hill. Look at all the ants running around." Sam frowned. Leo looked to see that Sam had crushed the ant hill, partially. The little ants were scurrying around. "Well," Sam said, "see what I mean. I'm not perfect. I make mistakes some-times. But the ants will rebuild this in no time. They're very hard workers."

"That's good," Leo replied. "And you did save those baby birds."

Sam smiled and put an arm around Leo's shoulders as they walked out of the patch of trees. "That's true," he replied. "What's your name?"

Leo looked up at his hero. "Leo," the boy answered.

Sam stopped and shook Leo's hand. "Nice to meet you Leo, I'm Sam."

"I know," Leo said. "You're Super Sam. Everyone knows you!"

Sam chuckled. "I guess that's true. Hey, I have to go, but I'll see you around, okay, Leo?" Leo nodded eagerly as the man smiled, waved and walked off.

Leo's mind was racing as he went home and to his pool for a swim. "I can't believe I met Super Sam in real life," he said to himself. "And that he fell – he made a mistake! I guess even superheroes make mistakes." Leo was happy to discover this. It meant it was okay he himself had made mistakes. Maybe he could still save animals just like Super Sam after all!

Even Princesses Make Mistakes

Trot – Trot – Trot

Along trotted Princess Lia's horse near the castle's stables, the princess riding atop. "Perfect riding Lia, wonderful!" Her riding teacher, Maggie, beamed at the princess.

"Thanks," Lia called out. She gave a little smile as she kept riding. She was happy about the compliment, but it also made her nervous. "What if I mess up? What if I'm NOT perfect?"

After her riding lesson, Lia went to the market in town with her best friend, Rachel. "Ooo, look at that dress Lia," Rachel's face lit up as she pointed to a fancy blue gown. "You should wear this to the party!" Lia gave a little smile but then sighed.

"Maybe... But Rachel, you know my problem. Maybe I shouldn't go to this party at all."

Rachel turned to her friend. "Just because you don't think you can sing? That's not a problem. I'm sure you're not that bad. And even if you are, it's all for fun. Don't worry so much!" But despite her best friend's words, Princess Lia chewed on her bottom lip. She was worried, she couldn't help it.

"It doesn't seem 'all for fun' to me," Lia told Rachel. "Not when I'm a horrible singer, and I'm supposed to sing all by myself in front of every single guest at the party!"

Rachel gave the princess a sweet smile. "Lia, you'll be fine. There's still five days until the party, and you have singing lessons every day until then, right?"

Lia nodded. "Yeah, starting this evening after dinner."

Rachel grinned and patted Lia's arm. "See, it's all good. Now let's see what shoes you can get with this dress!"

Lia ended up finding glimmering silver shoes to go with the dress and a lovely, sparkling tiara with blue jewels as well.

But she still headed home with a heavy heart. She heard whispers on the way home as she passed. One group of kids around her age even said under their breath, "Princess Lia is so beautiful and talented. She's good at absolutely everything! I wish I could be like her."

Lia felt the growing weight inside get bigger at these words. She tried to ignore it. But it didn't go away. In fact, it only grew worse at dinner. Lia was just washing down her bite of strawberry pie with milk when her dad, the King, smiled at her. "Lia, I heard from your royal tutor that you got one-hundred-percent on your science test. Well done, I'm very proud of you."

Lia swallowed the milk and shrugged. "It was nothing."

Her mom, the Queen, put a hand on her daughter's arm. "It wasn't nothing sweetie," her mom declared. "You also got top grades in math, history and English. You're so smart and talented... You're our perfect little princess." Lia gave a half-smile and quickly excused herself. The moment she left the dining room her mouth turned down. This wasn't helping her worries about the party. Not one bit.

"Ugh, and now I have my first singing lesson," she mumbled to herself as she went into the castle's beautiful music room. A kind looking young man smiled as Lia entered the room. "Good evening princess," he said. "I'm Mr. Limone, but please call me Pete.

And please stand up here for your singing lesson. We'll start with scale warm-ups."

Lia went to stand next to the teacher, her stomach twisting with knots. She'd only ever tried to sing on her own in the bathtub, in her room or in the woods by herself. "O… okay. Mr. Limone… I mean, Pete."

Lia went through scales together with the teacher while he played the piano. Since they sang together and with the piano, it wasn't so bad. "Maybe I can do this… really do this," Lia thought, hope rising like a bubble inside. But then Pete had her sing the song she'd chosen alone, and the bubble popped.

Though Pete Limone gave a kind smile afterwards, his eyes were wide with alarm and a little sympathy. His voice cracked here and there as he spoke. "Well, uh, now I know the level you're starting at – very useful. And you'll perform at the party in five days?"

Lia hung her head. "Yeah, that's right," she said glumly. He adjusted his glasses and stood taller, as if he were about to climb a giant mountain. "Well, you'll do just fine! Let's get to work."

And so, Lia practiced her song with him more that day, and the next. But on the third, fourth and fifth day, she pretended to be sick, and didn't tell her parents anything about this. The princess tried to practice one day in the woods by herself. Yet even the squirrels seemed to pull back and run away at the sound of her voice. Lia gave up and didn't practice at all the rest of the week.

"I might be making a big mistake," she told her reflection in the mirror that Saturday evening, right before the party. "But I don't care. Practicing was not helping. And it's all for fun anyway, like Rachel said, right?"

She gazed at herself and then nodded firmly, answering her own question. "Right!" With her new beautiful blue dress, silver shoes and tiara, she went down to the party in the castle's ballroom.

"Good evening princess Lia," an older lady with white curly hair wearing loads of jewels greeted her.

"Good evening," Lia said politely.

"You look just lovely," the lady gushed. "And I hear you'll be giving your first singing performance tonight. I can't wait!"

Lia forced her mouth to curve up. "Thank you."

But when she hurried away from the lady the smile was gone. "Maybe I can pretend to be sick before I have to sing. And maybe I should've practiced," she thought with a frown.

"Hey Lia," Rachel bounced up in a yellow dress that looked like sunshine. "You ready to sing? Are you nervous? You look kind of pale."

Lia shook her head. "I'm fine and let's not talk about singing. Let's just get some dessert and dance and have fun!"

Lia pushed down her nerves and really did have fun for the next hour, eating tiny chocolate and berry cakes, drinking sparkling fruit soda and dancing to the live orchestra that played. She nearly forgot about having to sing…until the music stopped, the lights lowered and the Queen came to the stage.

"And now, for the traditional princess performance, my daughter, Lia, will sing for us all. Lia, sweetie, come on up here!" The room burst into applause, clapping and cheering and buzzing with excitement. Lia could barely swallow as she walked up on the stage. Her mom smiled down at her then left her in the middle of the stage, alone. Lia twisted her hands in front, then behind as the hundreds of eyes stared, all glued to her!

It felt like a long time after the cheers stopped and everyone waited. "Just do it Lia, get it over with." So, the princess opened her mouth and started to sing. It was okay at first. Then she sang the wrong note…then another… and yet another. She pushed on, palms sweating and everything sounding like it was underwater. She was beyond nervous. Then she forgot the next line and stopped singing all together.

Everyone was completely still. Silence hung in the air like a heavy blanket. Her heart beat wildly as she looked around at the crowd. Seeing the shocked look on some people's faces, the worry on Rachel's face and then the frowns her parents gave her, the backs of her eyes started to prickle. That was it. She couldn't stay up there anymore. She couldn't be at the party. And she most definitely could NOT sing!

Tears running down her cheeks, she ran from the stage and out the ballroom door. Lia ignored her parents and best friend who called after her. She ran and ran down the castle hallway until she burst outside into a large garden. It was a beautiful place, especially in the rising moon and starlight from above. But Lia didn't notice. She threw herself down on a stone bench surrounded by rose bushes and sobbed.

"I'm not the perfect princess anymore. And everyone saw…" She put her face into her hands and cried some more. As the tears dried, she lifted her head, wiping at her cheeks with her mind made up. "It's going to be okay," she told herself. "I'll just move to another country and…"

But a girl's voice interrupted, "Please don't move away Lia," Rachel was smiling down at her. "What am I going to do without my best friend?"

Before Lia could answer, the King and Queen walked up. Lia couldn't even look them in the eye. Rachel gave her a quick hug and backed away so Lia's parents could get closer.

The Queen sat down next to her daughter. "Lia, I can see you're upset and embarrassed about making some mistakes during your song." Lia's insides turned, she felt sick. Her mom went on, "But why on earth would you want to leave us? Why are you crying so much?"

Lia's lower lip trembled as she answered, "I made too many mistakes. Everyone thought I was perfect – even you wanted a perfect princess. But I'm not perfect. And now everyone hates me, so I have to leave!" Her mom shared a look with her dad, even chuckling a little. Lia crossed her arms. "I don't see what's so funny about this," she grumbled.

"It's only funny because it's so untrue, Lia," her dad said, smiling.

"That's right sweetie, we love you no matter what," her mom smiled gently, putting an arm around Lia. "And we know you're not perfect, no one is."

Her dad nodded and knelt to give her a big hug, saying, "That's right. Even Kings and Queens like me and your mom are not perfect. Princesses aren't perfect either. Even princesses make mistakes." And with that, Lia let out a little laugh and hugged them both, knowing she was truly loved, mistakes and all!

Even Squirrels Make Mistakes

"What a hot day!" gasped Sasha Squirrel, draped over a tree branch. Her arms and legs dangled as she tried to cool off.

"It's so humid, too!" said her younger brother, Sol, flopping down near her. The two of them were expert builders and had spent all week creating a beautiful new treehouse in the deep part of the forest. There were just a couple of finishing touches left to do.

"The party is tonight," Sasha reminded Sol. "What a great way to introduce our new treehouse to everyone. Mom and Pop haven't even seen it yet!"

"I guess we'd better go over there and add the moss and leaves for a soft carpet," Sol said.

"And paint the door blue," Sasha added. Mom had told her the treehouse door must be painted blue. She didn't know why.

"I don't feel like finishing the tree house today," she thought to herself. She usually was a responsible squirrel, but today she felt so warm she just wanted to take it easy.

Suddenly, Jeremy Chipmunk came dashing past. "I'm going to play hide and seek with Randall!" he cried. "Come and join us."

Randall was a raccoon, and one of their good friends. "C'mon Sol," Sasha said, scampering after Jeremy. They all ran until they got to a sassafras bush. Suddenly, Randall jumped out at them, laughing. "Oh, you startled me!" Sasha laughed back.

For an hour, the four friends played hide and seek in the cooler shadows of the forest. Jeremy hid in a hollow log once. It took a long time to find him. Sol hid at the top of a very tall fir tree. That was another good hiding place. "You were hard to find," Jeremy told Sasha, who had tucked herself between two big rocks.

When it was Sasha's turn to look for her hidden friends, she couldn't find Randall. "I give up!" she called. A pile of leaves moved suddenly and out popped Randall. "That was a great hiding idea," Sasha said.

All this time, Sasha forgot about finishing the treehouse in time for the party that evening. As the sun rose higher, the day grew hotter. "Let's go swimming," Sasha suggested. Everyone agreed, and they all started toward the forest pond. Randall jumped in first with a big splash. Then Sasha and Sol jumped in the cool water. The three swam around and floated, cooling off for a good while. Jeremy only put his toes in the water. He didn't like to swim as much as the others.

All that morning while the friends played, Mom Squirrel was sealing envelopes with invitations for their relatives and friends. Each invitation said, "The blue door is the entrance to the new treehouse. Look for it in the deep part of the forest."

Pop Squirrel said, "Would you like me to take those to Owl for delivery?"

Owl delivered all the mail in the forest. "Sure. Thanks," Mom Squirrel replied. By afternoon, all the animals in the forest had received their invitations and were happily planning to attend.

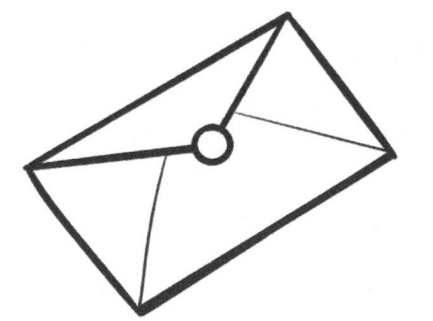

Back at the pond, Sol said, "I'm hungry!" And to Sasha he added, "We really should get to work on the treehouse."

"It's not done?" Randall asked. "What about the party?"

Sasha shrugged. "Oh, it'll be ready in time for that," she said airily. The friends went to dig up a near-by supply of nuts.

"I can't shell nuts," Randall said, so the others shelled the nuts for him, and he enjoyed eating the moist insides. After lunch, every-one was so sleepy they took a nap in a hollow tree. By the time they woke up, the sun was much lower in the sky.

"We'd better get to work, Sasha," Sol worried.

"Let's wait until dusk. It'll be cooler then," Sasha said. "How long does it take to put a couple coats of paint on the door? It dries fast in this heat, too."

"Well...okay," Sol agreed reluctantly. The animals decided to play freeze-tag. Randall made the funniest statue when he had to "freeze" balancing on one leg. As dusk settled in, crickets sang softly.

Finally, Sol and Sasha left for the treehouse. On the way, they gathered moss and leaves to make the soft carpet. "There! That looks and feels nice," Sol said, patting the last bit of moss into place on the floor of the main treehouse room. There were other smaller rooms too, plus two balconies, a rope ladder and tree swing. Now only the front door needed painting. Sasha looked in the work shed for paint.

"I know there was some paint in here. I think it's blue. Mom really wanted me to paint it blue," she said to herself. But all she could find was a can of purple paint. "It's too late to go to the hardware store," she told Sol, showing him the purple paint. "But this is close to blue. Red and blue make purple, right?"

"I guess so," Sol said. "It'll have to do, anyway."

The two squirrels busily painted the front door purple. It dried fast, and they added a second coat. "It looks nice," Sasha said as they stood back to admire their work.

As evening fell, a crescent moon lit the trees with silver. Fireflies filled the forest with twinkling lights. Many of Sasha and Sol's firefly friends came to light the tree-house from within. Mom and Pop arrived carrying loads of food and games. They didn't notice that the door was purple instead of blue. Sasha and Sol had propped it open so you couldn't see what color the front of it was. This also made it easier to bring in the food and games.

From all over the forest animals excitedly began heading to the party, even the ones who usually slept at night. Squirrels, chipmunks, lizards, skunks, birds, badgers and foxes all gathered together and flew, leapt or trotted toward the remote part of the forest.

Wyleen, a cardinal, flew ahead looking for the new tree-house. Soon she circled back. "I only see a treehouse with a purple door," she told the crowd.

Everyone stopped, wondering what to do. "Then it's not the right one," Badger said.

Fox spoke up, "I saw a hollow tree with a blue door a little while ago. Maybe that's what they meant by 'tree-house.'" The animals followed Fox to the blue door, and he knocked.

A surprised-looking opossum opened the door. "Hello?" he said wonderingly.

Fox said, "We thought this might be the treehouse we were looking for. Our party invitations say to look for a blue door. I'm sorry we disturbed you."

"We just moved here," the opossum said. "I'm Opossum."

"I'm Fox. Why don't you join us? It'd be a great way to meet your new neighbors!" Fox added, "If we ever find the right treehouse that is!"

Two small faces peeked out from behind Opossum. "Well…yes, I think that would be fun. Thank you!" he said. "This is Opo and Pom." Opossum, with Mom Opossum and the two little ones, joined the guests, and they all began searching for the treehouse again.

Back at the treehouse, the Squirrel family was confused.

"I wonder where everyone is?" Mom said. The delicious food was piled on log tables in the treehouse. The fire-fly lamps gave the room a soft glow. Games were ready, and the carpet was comfortable. But there were no guests.

"I took the invitations to Oliver Owl," Pop said. "He's very reliable. I'm sure everyone got theirs."

"I thought I put the right date and time down," Mom fretted. "And I said to look for the blue door."

Sasha opened her eyes wide. Then she looked down, feeling bad. "I'm sorry, Mom," she mumbled. "I knew you wanted the door blue, but I didn't realize it was part of the directions to the party. If I hadn't played in the woods all day, I'd have had time to go to the hardware store and get blue paint. I've spoiled the whole party!"

A tear rolled down her furry face. "What do you mean?" Pop asked.

Sasha said, "The door is purple. We were out of blue paint, so we used purple." She began to cry in earnest.

Sol said, "I should have insisted we work on the tree-house before we played."

Sasha sniffled, "You tried to warn me several times, Sol. It's all my fault."

The woods were still very silent, and the Squirrel family sat alone in the beautiful new treehouse. "Maybe they'll find us, after all," Pop said. "Don't feel too bad, Sasha. We all make mistakes. It's not the end of the world." But Sasha just cried and cried. If only she had endured a little heat and worked earlier, there would have been time to get the right color of paint. All Mom's and Pop's and Sol's work for the party had been for nothing. And their neighbors would be so disappointed.

Sol nibbled on an acorn. He was the only one with any appetite. Mom pricked up her ears. "What's that?" she asked. "I hear voices from far away." Soon the whole family could hear voices which were cheerful and excited. The voices came closer. The Squirrels went out on the front balcony to see. In the distance and coming closer were little lanterns, fluttering wings and the rustling of animal feet, and all the animals chattering happily.

Wyleen flew up to the Squirrels. "At first, we thought this was the wrong treehouse because the door wasn't blue. But we decided to check again, and now I see it is you, after all!"

"Welcome!" Mom smiled, "I'm so glad you found us. The door is purple by mistake, but it's all okay now! Come in and eat and play!" The rest of the animals came up the tree and rope ladders or just flew up.

Fox said, "This is Pop Opossum and Mom Opossum and Opo and Pom, our new neighbors. They do have a blue door, so we went there first."

Sasha was happy to see all the animals finally arriving, but she was still crying. "See," Mom said to her, "we all make mistakes, so don't feel bad. And this turned out to be a wonderful mistake, because now we can get to know our new neighbors, the Opossums!" Sasha smiled through her tears. Soon she and Sol were introducing Opo and Pom to Randall and Jeremy, and they all began to scamper around the whole treehouse, eating delicious food and playing party games.

After the fun and successful party, the treehouse door stayed purple, and the treehouse was called the House of the Purple Door. It really did look nice, and it became a popular gathering spot. And Sasha learned that mistakes are part of life and can even turn out for the best.

Even Mermaids Make Mistakes

"Oh, that's the perfect seashell for your outfit," Finn told her best friend, Luna. Luna was a mermaid child, a mer-girl, with long silvery hair, like moonlight. And since 'Luna' means 'moon,' her name fit perfectly. She also had a light purple tail with scales. Finn had been her best friend since she was a little mermaid and Finn was a baby dolphin. Finn smiled at Luna who looked in her coral-framed mirror. She had just put a large blue and pink striped shell in her hair.

"I think you're right," Luna told Finn. "It's perfect with my outfit. And it's very in style right now. Meg, Tiffany, Cole and Liam will think I'm sooo cool. Maybe they'll even let me play with them during recess!"

Finn's smile disappeared. "Why do you care what those mer-girls and boys think so much?" Finn asked.

"They're so cool and always have the latest trends and fashionable clothes and shells and things," Luna answered. "I'd love to be part of their group, so I'm cool too."

"But Luna, you're cool no matter what you wear," Finn insisted.

Luna shrugged as she grabbed her shell bag and turned around. "I don't think that's true. Now, I have to go, or I'll be late for mer-school. Let's play in the reef this afternoon?" Finn nodded and swam out of the room with her best friend. Finn left for dolphin school and Luna went to her mer-school.

She weaved into her level's classroom and sat in one of the bright coral-built chairs with a desk.

Her eyes darted around as she pulled out her notebook and squid-ink pen, ready to take notes. After a moment, she saw who she'd been looking for – Meg, Tiffany, Cole and Liam, the coolest kids in her level. Luna smoothed her silvery hair and made sure her blue and pink striped seashell was in place. She also straightened out her new ruffled purple shirt which looked like the white one Meg wore.

Luna eagerly watched as Meg led the other three into the classroom, passing right by. Meg didn't say a word to Luna. But Tiffany glanced down at her and said, "I like your hair-shell," and kept walking.

"Thanks!" Luna called after her, a little loudly.

The mer-boy sitting to Luna's left, Frank, adjusted his glasses and said, "They're so snooty." He nodded his head towards Meg, Tiffany, Cole and Liam.

Luna gave Frank a frown. "No, they're not, they're just cool." Then she secretly thought, "Not a nerd with no fashion like you, Frank." But she felt bad as soon as she thought this. Frank was nice, and she wasn't a mean mer-girl, even though she wanted to be cool and fit in so badly. Frank just arched one eyebrow and focused on the front of the room as the teacher came in.

Mr. Clark was the regular teacher for their level. For special subjects like Anemone Art and Oyster Orchestra they had other teachers. Mr. Clark kept his body in the front of class by swishing his tail back and forth. "Okay class," he said, "let's start with the Sea Creature Studies quiz. Frank and Luna, please help pass them out?" Luna and Frank swam to the front to help.

At recess that day, Luna hovered with her tail swishing near Meg, Tiffany, Cole and Liam. They were playing 'pass the pearl,' which involved throwing a huge pearl around like a ball—kind of like the human game called 'hot potato.' "Please invite me to play," the mer-girl thought. They glanced at her a few times. But they never asked. So, when Frank and his friend Izzy asked her to play jump-rope with long strands of seaweed, Luna agreed.

For most of the week, though Luna tried more and more to wear the right things, Meg and her group didn't ask her to play at recess. Thursday afternoon, after school, Luna went to the aqua lagoon to hang out with Finn. She had a pile of the latest Tail Trends, which showed very hip things to wear for both mer-girls and mer-boys. It was just the two of them at the lovely lagoon. "Look at these new kind of tail clips," Luna pointed to the picture in the magazine.

"I like their different shapes," Finn replied. "Especially the starfish and the seahorse ones."

Then Finn waved a flipper towards her school bag. "Oh, I almost forgot, I brought another fashion magazine for you," Finn told Luna.

Luna helped get it out of the bag and started to look through, her green eyes shining with excitement. "Ooo, I've never seen this one," the mer-girl exclaimed. "Thanks Finn!"

Finn made several happy high-pitched dolphin noises and said, "Your welcome!"

Luna looked through the pages of the magazine Finn had brought, called Fishy Fashion For All Underwater Creatures. Then she stopped on one page and studied it. "Wow, I really like the way this angel fish wrapped seaweed around her fins, kind of like a garland."

Finn looked too. "Yeah, I like it too. I've never seen that before."

Luna thought for a minute and then said, "I want to try it around my tail. What do you think?"

Finn nodded, her bottlenose moving up and down too, making little waves in the water. "I think it would look great!"

Luna put the magazine away. "Will you help me look for the right color seaweed now?"

"Of course, let's go!" Finn exclaimed.

Luna was about to start the search when her eyebrows came down. "Wait, I've never seen Meg or anyone wear seaweed around their tails. Maybe it's too different to wear to school?"

Finn shook her head. "Who cares if they haven't. You should wear whatever you want to, Luna!"

Luna swished her tail a few times then replied, "Okay, I guess you're right. Let's search." But she wasn't quite as excited now.

Luna and Finn had found the perfect light green seaweed in long strands to go with the light purple scales on her tail. So, the next day, she carefully wrapped it around her tail like a garland. She put her long silver hair into a long braid that hung down her right side. And she used a starfish barrette just above her ear in her hair.

"Okay, I think this looks good. I hope Meg and the others do too," she told her reflection. "And maybe they'll ask me to play 'pass the pearl' today."

She swam into Mr. Clark's class a little late that morning. As she went over to a coral chair in the back, she passed by Meg, Tiffany, Cole and Liam. All four of them looked at her and then at the seaweed around her long tail, ending at the fins on the bottom. One of Meg's eyebrows went up, and her mouth turned down. They all started whispering, but Luna couldn't hear what they said.

Her cheeks were hot by the time she sat next to Frank. "Oh no," she thought. "It didn't seem like they liked my new look – not at all!"

When Frank said, "Hey, neat seaweed on your tail. I've never seen that." Luna barely paid attention. She gave a little smile that quickly turned upside down. But maybe they just needed to talk about her new look more, then they'd start to like it.

Luna noticed other mer-girls and boys looking at her tail for the rest of the morning and through lunch. Some smiled and others just whispered. The silver-haired mer-girl wasn't sure what to think by the time recess came. Like always, she swam in place near Meg, Tiffany, Cole and Liam who played 'pass the pearl.' And her heart thumped hard when Meg actually stopped playing and swam over to her!

"You're Luna, right?" Meg asked without a smile.

"Um, yes, that's right," Luna answered.

Meg looked down at the seaweed around Luna's tail, then back up. "I just thought you should know that sea-weed-tail look is from ages ago, like over five years. No one wears that anymore, it's not cool at all. Just thought you should know." Without waiting for Luna to answer, Meg turned and finned her way back to her group.

All the blood drained from Luna's face as she stared after Meg. She went very pale. And then heat flooded back into her face, even to her ear-tips and scalp. She was about to swim away before the tears began to fall, but she heard one more thing first. Meg whispered loudly to Liam, Cole and Tiffany. "Such a fashion mistake!" Then Luna turned and swam as fast as she could out of the school area and to aqua lagoon.

Tears came out from her prickling eyes and instantly blended with the ocean water around her. "I can't believe I made such a fashion mistake, like Meg said," she told herself. "That magazine Finn brought must've been from five years ago! I hate this stupid seaweed!" As she slowed in the lagoon area, she ripped off the pretty light green seaweed from around her tail.

Then she pulled herself onto a sun-warmed, smooth rock in the ocean and put her face in her hands. Luna cried a bit more. The tears stopped but she still felt hurt inside. She looked up at the blue sky dotted with puffy white clouds. And then she looked at the sandy beach a little way in front of her. "I tried so hard, but I'll never fit in with Meg and her group," Luna told herself aloud. "I'll never be cool. And now I don't know how I'll ever go back to school after today!"

Just then, Finn spoke from the left of the rock, long nose out of the water, "What do you mean you don't know how you'll go back to school? What happened?" Luna then told her best friend about what Meg had said. Finn looked angry – at least as angry as a dolphin can look. "Meg is wrong Luna," Finn said. "That was really mean of her to tell you that. And, like I've said before, who cares what she thinks. You liked the look of the seaweed, so you wore it. Who knows, you could even make it 'cool' to wear again! Just do what you want. Be unique!"

65

Luna thought about this for a moment, but still wasn't sure. That weekend, she went with her parents and baby brother to a busy restaurant for dinner. She saw Frank and Izzy, who were best friends with their parents, just a few tables over. Frank and Izzy saw her too and swam over to the huge clam shell she sat in.

"Hey Luna," Frank smiled as Izzy said, "Hi!" Luna gave a half-smile, wondering if they'd heard about her fashion mistake on Friday. She knew they'd seen the seaweed but didn't know if they'd heard what Meg told her at recess.

"Hi Frank... Hi Izzy."

Izzy then moved her tail around and said, "Oh, Luna, by the way, I loved your seaweed style so much on Friday I found some for myself too!"

Luna's mouth fell open as she looked from Izzy's face to her green tail. It had reddish-brown seaweed wrapped around like a garland, just like Luna had done. And it looked really good! "Oh wow, that looks great Izzy," Luna said. Then she added, "But, well, Meg told me this look is old, from five whole years ago..."

Izzy shrugged her shoulders. "So what? I love it, and I'm glad you're bringing the look back!"

Frank nodded. "Me too, I'm going to look for brown seaweed to wear around my tail Monday!"

With that, they swam back to their table, leaving Luna gaping in shock. "Are Finn, Frank and Izzy right?" she wondered. "Should I just wear what I want and not care about what's 'in style' or 'cool?' Should I not care what Meg, Tiffany, Cole and Liam think?" She thought about it all through her spicy scallop dinner, and then all evening and night. By Monday morning, as she got ready for school, her mind was made up.

Luna was nervous when she swam into Mr. Clark's class that morning. She saw other mer-boys and girls looking at her and her tail. Most of them smiled. She was wearing some glittering silver seaweed she'd found in a magical sea cave early that morning. She thought it looked beautiful wrapped around her soft purple tail.

To Luna's surprise, she saw three mer-girls and four mer-boys wearing different colors of seaweed around their tails! Luna sat next to Frank, who had indeed found brown seaweed to wear around his tail. "What do you think?" Frank asked, pointing to his tail.

"It looks great," Luna told him honestly. When Meg and the others swam in, she gave Luna a long look. But Luna couldn't tell what it meant since Meg's mouth was in a straight line.

Luna had been amazed to see more and more mer-girls and boys wearing seaweed around their tails. She beamed with pride that she'd restarted a fashion trend from five years ago. But by recess, she felt nervous again. She watched Meg and the others play 'pass the pearl' for a minute, then went to play with Frank and Izzy instead. Luna jumped a little when someone tapped on her shoulder. She turned to see Meg.

"Hi Luna," Meg said with a little smile, "I... I'm sorry about what I said Friday. It was kind of mean. And I was wrong, seaweed around the tail isn't a fashion mistake at all. It's really cool. I love how your silver seaweed matches your hair!" Luna blinked at Meg, her mouth opening and closing several times.

Then Luna smiled. "Thanks!"

Meg added, "Do you think you could help me find some cool seaweed for my tail later today?"

Luna nodded eagerly. "Of course!"

Meg was about to turn but added, "Do you want to play 'pass the pearl' with us?" Luna couldn't believe it. She'd finally been asked to play with Meg, Tiffany, Cole and Liam. It was nice, but she didn't care quite so much.

So, Luna said, "Thanks, but I'm going to do jump-rope with Frank and Izzy today. Maybe another time."

"Okay, sounds good. And see you later!" Meg waved and swam back to her group. Luna smiled to herself for the rest of recess and the rest of the day.

Luna now knew she didn't need to be like everyone else to fit in. She was her own unique, one-of-a-kind mer-girl. And her fashion 'mistake' had turned out to be the coolest new underwater fashion trend in her entire mer-school!

Even Older Brothers Make Mistakes

"Oh wow, I like your painting," Cassi's art teacher, Ms. Ettinger said. "That's a great... um, bird and a tree, right?" Ms. Ettinger adjusted her thick-framed glasses, looking more closely at Cassi's painting. Cassi sighed.

"No, it's supposed to be a pig and a carrot he's going to eat," Cassi told her teacher.

Ms. Ettinger's eyebrows went up and then she quickly hid her surprise with a smile. "Well, you get an 'A' for effort at least. Keep practicing." The teacher patted Cassi's shoulder and went on to the next student in class.

"Ugh, why can't I be a super amazing artist like my brother?" Cassi thought to herself with a frown. It was true. Her older brother, Mike, was just as good at art as Cassi was bad at it!

That evening after dinner, Cassi, Mike, their parents and dog, Taffy, sat around the big living room. Her mom and dad played a board game while Taffy sat on the floor, chewing on her favorite bone. And Cassi sat near Mike who was perched on a stool at his tilted art desk. She tried to focus on her math homework but kept looking over at his painting.

"Is that for school?" Cassi asked him.

Mike dipped his brush into some silver paint. "Nope, it's for a town community contest," he told her, nose tilted up in pride. "I'll be competing with people of all ages." Cassi watched as he dotted the glittering silver over midnight blue on his canvas to make stars.

It was beautiful. And, unlike her painting, you could tell it was the night sky with what looked like a dragon mixed with clouds flying through. "Wow, that's cool," Cassi said. "It looks awesome, but why is there a dragon? And some other parts don't look totally 'real.'"

Mike glanced at his sister. "It's not supposed to be real, it's abstract art," he explained. "And this one is 'fantastique' art because it has a dragon – like 'fantasy,' which means make-believe."

Cassi nodded, wide-eyed. "Make-believe art? I wish I could paint stuff like that." Mike didn't say anything back, he just focused on making the stars. They really looked like they were 'alive' and twinkling.

Over the next four school days and into the weekend, Cassi watched as her brother worked carefully on his painting. He would work in the living room or kitchen or in his bedroom. Sometimes he even painted out in their backyard, looking up at the sky and studying the clouds or trees. It was Sunday evening when Cassi came out to watch as he painted in the yard.

"Why do those horses have long flowy bodies?" Cassi asked, pointing to some horses running along the ground of his painting.

"They're spirit horses – fantasy, or make-believe art, remember?"

"I remember," she said. "When do you have to turn it into the contest?" Mike finished a brush stroke of gray on one of the horse's tails.

"This Wednesday, so I've got three more days, plenty of time." He smiled widely.

Cassi watched for a little more before going inside and heading into her room. She pulled out a piece of paper and a pencil. "Maybe I can start with something easier, like drawing," Cassi mumbled to herself. "Maybe I'm really good with a pencil and I just don't know it."

She sat in her desk chair, took a big breath and got to work. "I can just draw my window with the trees beyond it," she thought. She drew a big rectangle and then smaller ones for the windowpanes. Then she drew the branches and leaves she could see through the window. When she was done, she looked at her picture.

The lines were all crooked and the leaves looked more like racoons' paw or something. She felt her heart sinking. "This is just awful," she told herself. "I can't even draw something simple with a pencil. It's not fair! Why can't Mike make a mistake sometimes – even one itsy-bitsy mistake in his art?!" Cassi crumpled up the piece of paper and threw it into her trash can.

Cassi felt a little bad about what she'd said – wanting her older brother to mess up. But she was jealous. The next day, that Monday afternoon, however, she wished she could take back her words.
Because Mike finally made a mistake with his art... a big mistake!

He was nearly done with his painting, working on it in the kitchen before dinner. Cassi was in the living room with her mom. "Cassi, sweetie, can you feed Taffy for me?" her mom asked.

"Sure Mom, I..." But Cassi was interrupted by a loud "AGGHH – NOOOO!" It came from her brother in the kitchen!

Cassi and her mom rushed in, their dog following along to see what had happened. "Mike, honey, are you okay?" their mom asked, eyebrows in a 'V' shape.

Mike looked from his painting up to his mom. "No, I'm not okay! I messed up and I can't fix it!"

He pointed a paintbrush, dripping with vivid orange paint, to his canvas. Cassi's heartrate sped up. She'd never seen her brother look so pale and upset.

Cassi and her mom rushed around to get a good look at Mike's painting. There, in the middle of the dragon's face and mouth, was a huge bright orange spot! It was dripping downward from the dragon and already starting to dry. "Oh no, honey," their mom said with a hand on Mike's shoulder. "You can just wipe it off right?" Mike, his face still as white as a ghost, grabbed a napkin and started to dab the orange spot.

Cassi watched, chewing her lip, as the orange just went deeper into the canvas, staining the dragon and the spots going down to the ground. Mike threw the napkin to the floor, eyes glistening with tears. "It's no use!" Mike yelled as he stood up. "There's no way to fix this, and I don't have time to do another painting before the contest! It's due the day after tomorrow!"

Opening her mouth, Cassi started with, "But Mike, maybe you can..."

Mike stopped his sister. "No, nothing will help Cass, don't even try!" And with that, he stormed out of the room, stomped up the stairs and slammed his bedroom door shut! Cassi stared after him, her stomach twisting. She felt like she might cry.

"Just let him cool off Cass," her mom said with a side-hug. "I'm sure your brother will figure something out."

Cassi and her mom looked at the painting – at the mistake – again. Then Cassi followed her brother's path and went upstairs, slamming her bedroom door shut. Hot tears started to fall down her cheeks. She flopped onto her bed and covered her eyes with her hands. "This is all my fault. I jinxed my own brother," Cassi cried to herself. "I wanted him to make a mistake and he did. And now he can't enter the contest and win!"

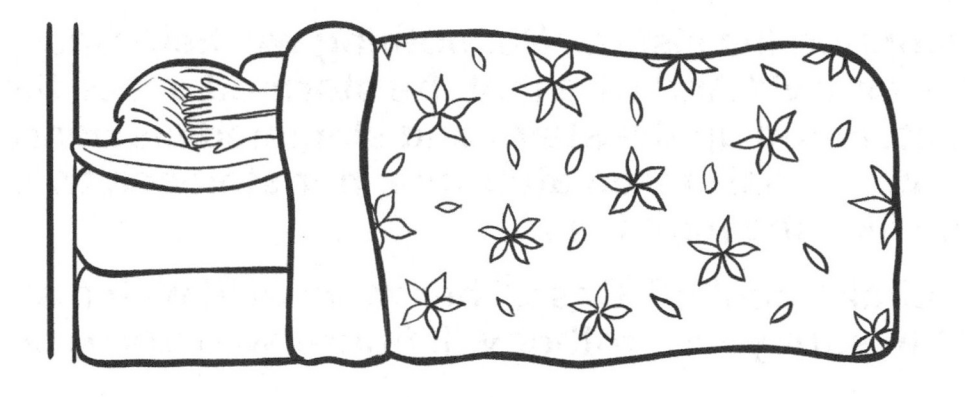

She cried a little more and then wiped her tears. Heading out into the hall, she tiptoed up to Mike's bedroom and listened through the door. She could see his lights were off under the door and heard angry music playing. She sighed and went back into her room until dinner. Mike didn't come down for dinner and her parents just let him stay in his room. He stayed there through the night and Cassi went to bed very unhappy.

The next day, Mike dragged his feet all day, his mouth turned down. "Mike, Mom made your favorite dinner," Cassi smiled at him. He shrugged, not even looking at her. Taffy came in, tail wagging, nudging Mike's hand. He gave her one pat and pulled his hand back into his lap. He was quiet all through dinner.

After dinner, dessert and homework, Cassi wandered to the backyard where she'd seen Mike go. He was staring at his painting on his art desk. "You didn't throw it out?" Cassi asked as she walked up.

Mike shook his head. "No." It was silent for a minute.

"I think it was my fault," Cassi said suddenly, all in one breath. "I was jealous you're so good at art and I'm horrible, so I wished you would make a mistake!"

A few tears trickled out and Mike gaped at her. "What? This isn't your fault little sis," his face softened. "It was my fault. My hand shook because I was nervous about adding orange to the scales and I made the mistake – all on my own. It wasn't your fault at all!" Mike put an arm around her shoulder.

"You r… really don't think it's my fault?" Mike shook his head.

"Not at all Cass. And by the way, you're good at so many things besides art. Like math, singing and playing soccer."

Cassi hugged her brother and then stood next to him. Both of them looked at the painting. Then Cassi got an idea. "Hey, you know, that orange there kind of looks like fire coming from the dragon's mouth, going down onto the ground."

Mike blinked several times as he stared at the orange mistake. Then his face lit up with hope. "Cassi, you're right. I might be able to change that orange into fire, gently floating down onto the horses. A magic fire!"

Cassi beamed as her brother dashed inside to get his paints. Over the next few hours, Mike worked and worked, turning the orange 'mistake' into magical dragon's fire. Cassi got too tired to stay and watch and went to bed. She slept better than she had in days, knowing it wasn't her fault. And also knowing she'd helped Mike save his painting.

It was Friday of that same week when the contest winners were going to be announced. Cassi, Mike, Taffy and their parents gathered at a small outdoor park that had a stage and gazebo. "I'll bet you've won, or at least come in the top three," their dad told Mike.

"We'll see. I hope so," Mike said, eyes on the man who came to the stage's microphone.

The next minute, the man's voice boomed out over the medium crowd gathered around. "Good afternoon. I'm Mr. Smith, President of the Community Art Foundation." And Mr. Smith went on and on about how the foundation got started and blah, blah, blah.

"Hurry up and tell us who won!" Cassi thought, clasping her hands.

As if hearing her thoughts, Mr. Smith then said, "And now it's time to announce the top three winners of this year's contest." Cassi and her parents gave Mike a smile before looking towards the stage. "In third place is Hettie Johnson." Claps and cheers sounded as Hettie, a gray-haired woman, went to the stage and took her trophy. "In second place, we have our youngest artist in the contest, Michael Hollister!"

Cassi, Mike and their parents cried out with cheers! Even Taffy barked with excitement. Mike hurried to the stage to get his trophy. Cassi didn't even hear who got first, it didn't really matter to her. Her brother almost hadn't even entered the contest at all. And now he'd won second prize! Cassi and her parents clapped and cheered for long after Mike had been called up.

A little later, the Hollister family sat at a booth in their favorite diner for a celebration dinner. "We're so proud of you, son," Dad smiled as Mike sipped his chocolate milkshake.

"That's right," Mom agreed. "Winning second as the youngest contestant, and after you thought you'd ruined your painting too."

Mike nodded and looked at Cassi. "It was Cassi's idea to turn the orange into dragon's fire. And the judges even told me they especially liked that part of the painting!"

His little sister grinned widely. "Really? That's awesome," she said. "And I never knew it, but I guess even older brothers – even you – make mistakes."

Everyone laughed at this, thinking Cassi was being cute. But she was serious. It was a nice thing to know he wasn't the perfect artist.

"That's true," Mike said. "And even 'mistakes' can turn out to be something more amazing than it would've been without messing up. I wouldn't have added the magic fire if I hadn't made the mistake." And with that, everyone nodded, and continued chatting happily as they finished their special dinner.

Even Star Athletes Make Mistakes

"Goaaall!!!" shouted the soccer announcer from the TV in front of Gilbert and his friend Tom.

"Wow, that was amazing!" Gilbert, usually called Gil, exclaimed.

"I know, Marco never misses a penalty shot," Tom agreed. Gil smiled as he looked from the basement TV screen to his friend. "Marco hasn't missed a single penalty shot since he joined the Tigers two years ago." Gil was an expert on the entire local soccer team of their city. And he was especially an expert on Marco, one of the Tiger's star players.

Gil put a handful of popcorn in his mouth, chewed and swallowed. Then he said, "I'm going to put in extra practice at shooting goals and penalty shots for our big game this Saturday." Tom nodded.

"Me too, it's our first big game and I want to win!" Gil and Tom gave each other a high-five. Then they continued watching the Tigers, Gil's eyes glued to Marco anytime he was on the screen.

That evening, Gil thought he'd get a head start on practicing. He went out to the back yard with his soccer ball. Their yard was a nice rectangular shape with a fence and a soccer goal in the back. The sun was just starting to go down, so the air was perfect – not too hot or cold. And, most importantly, there was still enough light to see for his goal practicing.

"It's the very last minute of the game," Gil said to himself as if he was the TV soccer announcer. "And the star player, Gilbert Gomez, is approaching the goal!" As he said this, Gil dribbled the ball with his feet towards the goal. He pretended there were other players trying to steal the ball from him. So, he moved quickly left, then right, and then he was free to shoot on goal!

"And he kicks…" Gil said as he drew his foot back and wham, he kicked the ball with the side of his foot, straight at the goal. The ball sailed through the air and went into the lower left corner of the net. "And he scores – gooooooaaal!" Gil threw his hands in the air and ran in a little circle to celebrate.

Suddenly someone clapped from behind him. "Nice goal Gilly," his older sister, Gloria, said. "Are you being your own soccer announcer?"

Gil turned to look at his sister, who was much taller than him. His cheeks went a little pink. "Uh, yeah I was kind of talking to myself."

She ruffled the top of his head with her hand. "That's cool, I like doing that too when I practice on my own."

His sister wasn't a soccer player but was an awesome volleyball player. She was pretty good at most sports, including soccer.

"Hey, you want me to practice with you?" Gloria asked.

"Sure, you can be defense while I try to make a goal," Gil said excitedly. "And can we practice penalty shots? I want to be as good as Marco from the Tigers!"

His sister laughed and playfully shoved his arm. "As good as Marco, huh? Well, let's see what we can do."

She practiced with him for almost an hour. Gil had made a few regular goals and two penalty shots. He felt good about this. But still, he needed to practice more. There were only four days until the big game on Saturday.

That week Gilbert practiced extra hard at the community youth soccer league practices. His team's name was the Hamsters. Gil really, really wished they had a cooler name, like the Tigers. Tigers were fierce. And hamsters were, well…not fierce. But he decided to let it go since he was at least on a soccer team. And he worked with all his heart on his team, at drills, practice games and penalty shots.

He felt good about how he did. But he wanted to be even better for Saturday. So, he practiced with his dad, mom and Gloria Friday evening and with Tom on Saturday morning before the big game. Right before the game, as Gil got dressed in his soccer jersey and cleats, he looked at the poster of Marco on his bedroom wall.

"I'm going to be as good as you today, Marco," he told the poster. "And one day, when I'm old enough, I'll be a star player on the Tigers too!" And with that, he was off to the game with his mom, dad and sister. It was finally happening!

The first half of the game went okay. Neither team had scored any goals. But Gil, Tom and the other Hamster team players were doing a good job. Their passes were aimed well. And they had several good attempts to make goals, though none had gone in just yet. In the second half, now with ten minutes left in the game, it happened. The Hamsters got to take a penalty shot, and the coach chose Gilbert to do it!

His heart beat hard against his chest. His stomach was flip-flopping like crazy as he stood back and to the left of the soccer ball. The crowd and other team members were cheering wildly. "Come on Gil!" he heard his mom and dad call out.

"Just like we practiced little bro!" his sister Gloria shouted.

Gil closed his eyes, remembering kicking the penalty goals into the net when he and Gloria practiced. "You can do it, just like before," he thought to himself. "Just like Marco." He opened his eyes, focused on the ball and ran towards it. His leg came back and WHOOSH! He kicked the ball hard. He watched, eyes wide as the ball flew through the air and then... It missed! It bounced off the left edge of the goal post and onto the grass!

Gil felt his stomach sinking, a wave of shame going through his insides. He looked over at his parents and Gloria who frowned. And then at his coach and other team members who also looked unhappy. "I can't believe I missed," he thought miserably. The game went on but Gil was too upset to play really well.

As the other team took the ball down towards the Hamster's goal, Tom ran next to Gil. "It's okay Gil, shake it off. No big deal!" Gil tried to smile and nod but couldn't.

There were only two minutes left, and Gilbert still felt horrible. Still, when the other team came towards their goal with the ball, Gil tried to block them. He stole it from the other player dribbling the ball.

Gil then passed the ball to the left…right into the feet of an opposing team player! "Thanks!" the boy told him with a big grin. Gil watched, stomach sinking even more, as the player kicked the ball towards the Hamster's goal, and it went in! "Gooall!" the boy exclaimed as his team members came to cheer.

Gil looked over at the scoreboard in misery. "One to zero, they're going to win," he thought as he dragged himself back to his position.

And then another player on the Hamsters, Don, went by and said, "You really messed this game up Gil! Now we're going to lose, because of you!" Gil left the game that day in tears. No matter how Tom, his coach, parents or Gloria tried to cheer him up and say it was 'okay,' he felt down in the dumps.

All week Gil felt this way. He went to practices but didn't enjoy it. In fact, he wanted to quit playing soccer for good. "I'll never be like Marco, not even close," he told himself in the hallway at home Friday evening.

"Don't be so hard on yourself honey," his mom said as she came by. "It was your first big game. And we have a surprise for you that might help cheer you up. We got tickets to see the Tiges play tomorrow!"

***

It was the second half of the Tiger's game, and Gil was having fun despite his down-in-the-dumps mood. The stadium was huge and filled with Tiger's fans where he sat. He had a hot dog, popcorn and ice cream while watching Marco and the others in real life. It really was exciting. "Oh, look Gil," his dad said, "Marco's up for a penalty shot!"

Gil sat taller in his seat, eyes on Marco. He watched, heart pounding, as Marco ran towards the ball and kicked. Then the unthinkable happened. Marco missed! The crowd was in an uproar, more surprised than angry. Gilbert sat there blinking in shock. "No way did he just miss a penalty shot!" Gil finally said.

"He did," his mom said. "But look, he's already back in playing."

Gil looked and saw that Marco was playing, and even smiling. And then, Gil was in for even more surprises after the game. The Tigers had still won and now Marco was being interviewed with a microphone so everyone could hear. "What about missing that penalty shot? What happened?" the man asked him.

Marco shrugged. "I just made a mistake, that's all. Everyone makes them and it's okay."

Gil leaned forward in his seat as Marco went on. "The important thing is to just shake the mistake off and keep playing. The really important thing is to have fun while playing soccer – that's why I play." Then the interview ended, and Marco went into the locker room.

Gloria, who was there too, leaned towards Gil, "See, even Marco, a star athlete, makes mistakes!" Gil nodded and smiled.

And after that, he felt much better and had more fun practicing that week. The next Saturday, the Hamsters had another big game. The same mean team player from before went by Gil in the beginning. "Don't mess it up for us this time!" Don said.

Gilbert just shook his head and said, "It's okay to mess up. Even Marco in the Tigers missed a penalty shot." Before the boy could answer, Gil ran off with Tom to get in his position.

It was the second half and the score was zero-to-zero. Gil ran as fast as he could to try and stop a player from scoring. But Gil tripped and landed on his stomach in the grass! "Oof!" Gil cried out. Tom gave him a hand up, just as the player made a goal against the Hamsters. Gil started to feel that horrible feeling inside. But then he remembered Marco.

And like Marco, Gil shrugged it off, smiled and kept playing. At one minute to the end of the game, Gil had a chance to score. Tom passed the ball to him and he was right in front of the goal. He grinned and kicked. Whoosh!! The ball went in the air and... It landed right in the net! "Gooaaal!" Tom cried with other team members as they came up.

Gil blinked in surprise. Then beamed and cried, "Gooaall!" He'd scored! Everyone cheered and the Hamsters ended up not losing but tying the game. His parents took him and Tom out for ice cream afterwards to celebrate. He had scored his first goal in a real game. But most importantly, Gil had fun!

Imprint

Contact:

KMU Media GmbH, Rathausstraße 35, 74613 Öhringen

Cover:

99designs.com